For Gaia

A Random House Australia book
Published by Random House Australia Pty Ltd
Level 3, 100 Pacific Highway, North Sydney NSW 2060
www.randomhouse.com.au

Penguin
Random House
Australia

First published by Random House Australia in 2015

Random House Books is part of the Penguin Random House group of companies
whose addresses can be found at global.penguinrandomhouse.com.

National Library of Australia
Cataloguing-in-Publication Entry

Author: Bound, Samantha-Ellen, author.
Title: Broadway baby
ISBN: 978 0 85798 903 1 (pbk)
Series: Silver shoes; 5
Target Audience: For primary-school age
Subjects: Musicals – Auditions – Juvenile fiction
         Auditions – Juvenile fiction
Dewey Number: A823.4

Cover illustration by J.Yi
Internal illustrations by Sarah Kate Mitchell
Cover design by Kirby Armstrong
Internal design by Midland Typesetters
Printed in Australia by Griffin Press, an accredited ISO AS/NZS 14001:2004
Environmental Management System printer

Random House Australia uses papers that are natural, renewable and recyclable
products and made from wood grown in sustainable forests. The logging and
manufacturing processes are expected to conform to the environmental regulations
of the country of origin.

Broadway Baby

SAMANTHA-ELLEN BOUND

RANDOM HOUSE AUSTRALIA

Chapter One

Belated birthday presents are the coolest.

This was the best one I'd ever received: better than my week-late trip to the Gold Coast on my eighth birthday; better even than the pre-order voucher for the whole series of *Dance Moms* when I turned ten.

My eleventh birthday was a few weeks ago. I'd had a party and everything, but now it was time to experience Mum and Dad's present:

a yummy dinner in the city with the biggest, most delicious sundae I'd ever had and, finally, I was about to watch a real, professional musical – something I'd dreamt about for years.

Mum and I had two tickets to see *42nd Street* at the Performing Arts Palladium in the big city!

I guess you have to know a bit about me to see why I was so excited. My name's Ellie, I'm a dancer and I've been working on becoming a 'triple threat' for a while now. A triple threat means you can sing, dance and act. So not only do you get way more opportunities, but you also get to do musical theatre.

And I love musical theatre! I've been going to my dance school, Silver Shoes, since I was a tiny, and my favourite style has always been jazz. But my teacher, Miss Caroline (who also owns the school), encouraged me to try musical theatre because I am 'very dramatic and expressive when I dance'. Our musical theatre teacher at Silver Shoes is called Billie, and she started giving me singing lessons. Then, I guess, I fell in love.

I'll never love any style as much as jazz, but musical theatre sure comes a close second. Don't get me wrong – I still have big dreams about being a famous dancer or choreographer and appearing in the video clips of pop stars. Maybe I'll even be a pop star myself!

But lately the stage has been calling me. Just thinking about it makes my fingers and toes tingle. I imagine how my acting will make people cry, and how my singing will fill the theatre and make the audience's hearts swell.

For a minute I will feel larger than myself, Eleanor Charlotte Irvin, and be part of something greater and more fabulous.

It's the same feeling I had now, as Mum and I weaved our way through all the people at the Performing Arts Palladium. Bodies were packed into the foyer and up the stairs, and everything smelt like toilet spray perfume and peppermint mouthwash. Mum and I had to go totally ant style, weaving our way in and out of arms and legs, and dodging the drops flung from people's champagne flutes while they laughed loud enough to burst our eardrums.

I mean, great that they're enjoying themselves, but I need my eardrums or I'll never be able to sing properly. I don't want my career sabotaged before it's even begun.

'Welcome,' the usher said to us at the door. He had a moustache drawn on with eyeliner and talked with an American accent like in gangster movies. His slicked hair had about half a tub of gel holding it back. 'How you two ladies doing tonight?'

'Just fine, thank you,' said Mum. She looked around at everyone and winked at the usher. 'Even better when we can breathe.'

'Why breathe when you can sing?' The usher shrugged. 'My name's Mikey, pleased to meet you.' He glanced down at me. 'And you, princess? You look like a leading lady in the making.'

I gave him a big smile and did a little curtsy so my glittery pink dress floated out. 'My name's Ellie,' I said. 'One day, I will be.'

'A princess or a leading lady?' The usher grinned.

'Both,' I said, flicking my blonde curls over my shoulder.

'Big aspirations, this one,' Mum chuckled, giving one of my curls a playful tug.

Mikey laughed. 'Maybe next time I'll be working the door for one of your shows.' He checked the tickets Mum was holding. 'Tonight you two will be seated on the mezzanine level. It's just up the stairs to the right. Enjoy. You'll see me around at interval.' He gave my nose a friendly tap. 'Maybe we can have a dance-off,' he said. 'Whaddaya think, angel?'

'I think you better be prepared to lose,' I said.

He laughed and so did Mum.

'Oh golly,' she said. 'Come on, Ellie, before you go and make me fetch your jazz shoes.'

She took my hand and we headed up the grand staircase, ready to watch the show.

Chapter Two

The theatre was *huge*.

Mum and I came to the top of the stairs and walked down the row to our seats. We were at the front of the mezzanine level, which is like a balcony, so you sit up high and look down onto the performance.

Curved stairs with gold balustrades led up to the stage and red velvet curtains – the lushest I'd ever seen – hung down either side.

There were lights along the walls of the auditorium that looked like old-fashioned gaslights, very dim but bright enough to see the shadows of people leaning over to whisper to each other or settle themselves in their seats. There was a buzz of excitement.

My heart felt dazzled by it all. It was like I'd stepped back in time and my insides went all glittery, the same way they do right before I'm about to go on stage myself.

I knew this was where I belonged.

'Stop squirming, Ellie,' said Mum, looking in her bag for some gum. 'There's people behind us, honey.' But I couldn't help it, I had to look everywhere and take everything in.

When the lights finally went down, the most spectacular hush fell over the audience as they waited for the show to start. I imagined how it would be standing on the other side of the curtain.

From the minute the opening chords of the first *42nd Street* song rang out, I was hooked. The story was set in something called the 'Great Depression' and it was about a young girl who arrives in New York, makes her way into the chorus line, and eventually lands the leading role in a big musical. Then she has to deal with falling in love and an older star who doesn't want to be upstaged by the latest 'it' girl.

There was heaps of dancing, but all the songs either went along with the story or moved the plot forward. Every single performer was beautiful and talented and had these pin-curl hairstyles, which made them look so glamorous. I made a note to try it out for school assembly next week (it was my turn to be the host, so I wanted to stand out).

The best part was that all the performers were equally as good at singing, dancing and acting. A lot of the dancing was tapping, which isn't really my thing, but *42nd Street* just about changed my mind. It was like the dancers were creating music with their feet, and the rhythms were so catchy and clever.

Costume and set changes rolled by and I was so entranced by the world on stage that Mum had to pull me back because I was leaning so far forward I almost toppled over the balcony.

But the stage and the songs were calling to me. They were saying, '*Come on down, Ellie – light up the stage with us! We need a girl just like you.*'

By the time the end rolled around and the cast were taking their bows, I felt like I'd just experienced magic. The real world seemed fake and boring, while the world on stage was in my blood.

I stumbled down the stairs with Mum

and almost ran into Mikey, the usher from before.

'Ahhh,' he said, reaching out a hand to steady me. One side of his eyeliner moustache had slightly smudged. He winked at Mum. 'She's got that look. There's no going back now.'

Mum laughed. 'She was born with that look.'

'So was I, once,' said Mikey.

But I barely heard, because I was walking somewhere up in the clouds. I was in musical theatre heaven. It had never been clearer what I was supposed to do.

Chapter Three

'And then they tapped on these coins and the coins lit up,' I whispered to my best friend, Paige.

We were lined up in the corner of the studio at Silver Shoes, waiting for our turn to do travelling exercises. I was trying to fill her – and our other two close friends, Riley and Ash – in on *42nd Street*.

'And the song was really catchy, it went like this –' I sang it, quietly of course, just under the music Miss Caroline had been playing, but Paige grinned at me.

'Wow, Ellie, you're getting really good,' she said.

'Posé turns,' Miss Caroline called out. 'Remember, spot that blue cross in the far corner, and keep the extended leg straight. Jasmine and Tove, you first.'

Jasmine and Tove always go first in travelling steps. Show-offs. Jasmine is one of the best dancers at Silver Shoes, and my number one competition. In the personality stakes, though, she loses. Tove just does whatever Jasmine wants.

They launched into their posé turns, and Miss Caroline followed them across the floor, her eyes never leaving their legs.

'Lovely, Jasmine,' Miss Caroline called out. 'Better, Tove – but pull up, pull up!'

'There was this other part,' I whispered to my friends excitedly, 'when they were in a carousel and there were these projections that made it look as if they were moving along, like trees and buildings going past, and they kept peeking out of the carriage curtains. It was so funny. I think the song was called "Shuffling Off to Buffalo".'

'Ellie, we're next,' Paige whispered to me.

I closed my mouth and lined up next to her. We took off across the floor in our posé turns. I love it when Paige is my partner in travelling steps. It's like looking in a mirror – we always keep so in sync.

Miss Caroline travelled with us across the floor, clapping on the down beat so we'd get the rhythm right.

'Lovely, girls,' she called. 'Paige, just watch you keep your shoulders down when you turn.'

'Ugh,' Paige said as we reached the other end of the studio and took a few steps to shake off the dizziness. 'You'd think with all the ballroom I've been doing my stupid shoulders would stay down.'

We watched Riley and Ashley posé across the floor. Riley, of course, looked like she was already dancing in some professional corps de ballet. Ash was improving too, but because she had so much energy she kept overstepping on the extended leg and putting herself off balance. You should see her dancing hip hop, though – then you'll know where all that energy goes!

Ash made a face as she lined up behind me and Paige. 'Ugh, Ellie,' she said, flicking her bangs off her forehead. 'I'm so dizzy I'm seeing three of you.'

'Sounds like your lucky day,' I said. 'So anyway, while they were in the carriages, there was another group at the front doing a tap sequence, and oh gosh, there was not one tap out of tune.' I turned to my best friend. 'Paige, why have you never told me how amazing tap is?'

Paige is well known for doing just about every style of dance. 'I did try,' she admitted. 'But you were too obsessed with jazz and how many fouettés you could do.'

Riley smiled. 'Doesn't sound like Ellie.'

'It's called being passionate,' I defended myself, although I knew they were only teasing. 'But in this Shuffling Buffalos song, they . . .'

'Quiet while you're waiting,' Miss Caroline called to us, without taking her eyes off Bethany and Brooke, the last two poséing across the room. 'Good, girls! Okay let's do fan kicks: the arm goes the opposite way to the leg, keep the core strong.' She demonstrated, before turning back to us. 'Remember, long walks between kicks – the aim is to travel. Jasmine and Tove, you first.'

'I'll tell you all later,' I whispered to my friends.

'Can't wait,' said Riley.

When class was finally over, I'd thought of a million more things about *42nd Street* that I just had to share. I bounded down the hallways of Silver Shoes to the change room, bursting with excitement.

That's when it happened.

Like a sign from the dancing gods.

On the Silver Shoes noticeboard: a flyer.

The Bayside Choral Society, with assistance from the Silver Shoes Dance School, are proud to present: Auditions for Mary Poppins: the Musical. *Can you sing, dance, tap and act? We want you! Children welcome!*

There was more written underneath, but that was all I needed to see.

Because the important thing was:

It was time for my musical theatre debut.

Chapter Four

I had a quick look round before reaching up to snatch the flyer off the wall.

Then I ran off in search of Billie, our musical theatre teacher.

She wasn't in studios one or two (they are our main studios, in the church that Silver Shoes is built from), but she was in the hall out the back, where most of the drama and musical theatre classes are held. Billie once told me it has better acoustics.

I saw her hair – which was coloured red, green and yellow, and bound up in a scarf – through the window in the door.

'Billie!' I said, pushing it open. 'I need to . . .'

I stopped.

'Hello there, Ellie,' said Billie, turning round, the bracelets on her arm jangling. Then she faced back to the small drama class she was obviously teaching. It was the seniors, and they were all looking at me like they didn't know whether to think I was cute or crazy. 'Now that's what I call a dramatic entrance,' said Billie, winking at them. 'How can I help you, Miss Irvin?' she asked me.

'Sorry, Billie,' I whispered, hiding the flyer behind my back. 'I really need to talk to you.'

'Well, lovely, if you can wait for two minutes while I finish with this class, I'm all yours.'

'Great. I'll just wait outside.' I turned to go and then remembered the manners Mum always goes on about. 'Sorry for interrupting,' I said to the class.

'Great voice projection,' said one girl, and I flushed and tiptoed out, taking extra care to close the door quietly, like that would make up for the obnoxious way I'd stormed in.

Those two minutes were the longest of my life! I paced up and down the corridor outside. It was the newest part of Silver Shoes, having only been built a few years ago to connect the hall to the main studios.

My eyes kept darting back to the flyer. *Mary Poppins*. Bayside Choral Society with the assistance of Silver Shoes. And then the information in the fine print: *Looking for triple threats to audition for main roles and a junior chorus. Performed at the Entertainment and Convention Centre.*

It sounded perfect.

Except for the part that said you needed to be able to tap.

I'd given up tapping when I was still in juniors because I wanted to focus on jazz (actually, Mum made me; I would have kept doing it, otherwise). Sure, I remembered the basics – toe heels and shuffles, slaps and stamps. But I knew I was rusty.

Would that ruin my chances of getting in? This could be my big break!

'Billie!' It burst out of me as soon as she had opened the door. 'Look!' I thrust the flyer at her.

She took a long look and her lips curved into a smile. '*Mary Poppins*,' she said. 'Yes, I know.

I put the flyer up myself!' She did a quick little sequence with her feet singing 'A Spoonful of Sugar', which is a song from the musical.

'Are you choreographing it?' I asked.

'Only the jazz parts,' Billie said. 'Not the tapping. Bayside Choral got someone else to do that. He's a teacher at Dance Art.'

'I want to try out!' I exclaimed.

'Well, that's super cool, girlfriend,' said Billie, handing the poster back to me. 'You've come a long way since you first started classes with me a few months ago. I definitely think you're up to it.'

'What will I have to do at the auditions?' I asked. (I HATE auditions.)

'Hmm,' said Billie, 'there'll be a couple of group dance auditions. Then you'll have to sing a number with piano and backing music for the director and the musical director, perhaps read a scene or two in a British accent. Can you do that?'

'Of course I can,' I said, ripping off the accent from all the movies I'd watched. 'And tapping? Will I have to tap?'

'Sure will,' said Billie. 'But I wouldn't get too stressed out about that. Even if you're not the best, as long as they see you're giving it a red hot go it should be fine.'

'Maybe I could do a tap class with you?' I blurted. 'Before the auditions. You know, the one Paige is in? Just to see if I'll go all right? I don't want to be good at everything else and be let down by lousy tapping.'

Billie gave a big, throaty laugh like it had blossomed right out of her heart. 'We couldn't have that,' she said. 'Yes, come along to the next tap class. Do you need to check with your parents first?'

'It'll be fine,' I said quickly.

Even if it wasn't, I would make it fine. I *had* to do the tap class. My musical theatre career depended on it!

'Okay, honeybee,' said Billie. 'We'll see you with taps on Thursday.'

I gave her a big confident smile, thanked her and then ran off, feeling like jellybeans were jumping around in my body.

As I passed by the noticeboard I thought about keeping the poster so no one else would see it and audition. My chances of getting in would be so much better. But at the last minute I quickly pinned it back up. If I got in, I wanted to earn my place.

It was time to start step-toe-heeling again.

Chapter Five

Heel, heel, heel, heel.

Toe, toe, toe, toe.

Shuffle, shuffle, shuffle, shuffle.

Slap ball change, slap ball change, slap ball change, slap ball change.

'I think I've got it,' I whispered to the back of Paige's head.

She turned around at the barre and gave me a quick smile before switching to do all the steps on her left. 'Unfortunately it gets a little harder than this,' she whispered.

'What?' I said, because the sound of twenty kids tapping can get pretty loud.

'It gets harder than this,' she repeated, louder. 'But you're a natural, Ellie, you'll be fine.'

So far I was breezing through my trial tap class. I was lined up with other kids, doing warm-ups in unison. What a terrific sound! It made me remember *42nd Street*, and I got so excited that I mucked up the timing on my steps.

Focus, Ellie, I told myself. *You're here to learn and to see how quickly you can master this tap thing. You can dream of fame and fortune later.*

Lucky I did focus, because things got harder pretty much straight away. Next we faced the barre and Billie yelled out, 'Pick ups!'.

A double pick up was a step where you had to brush back with both feet and land on the balls of your feet. Then Billie had us do trenches — where it took everything I had not to fall forward onto my face — and then wings, which was one of the most uncoordinated experiences of my life.

As if that wasn't enough, then we went around the room doing them all individually so Billie could listen to what kinds of sounds we were making.

I started to feel hot. For once, I didn't want the spotlight to be on me.

'Ellie,' said Paige, giving my hand a squeeze. 'You might be thinking too much about it. When I first started learning tap I used to just focus on the sounds the different steps make, and let my feet copy them. Sometimes if you get caught up in stuff like what this leg is doing and where that foot is supposed to go, you mess yourself up. You have a really good understanding of rhythm, so maybe focusing on the sound is what you should do.'

I thought about that. I closed my eyes and listened to the beats of the taps: how some brushed, some scraped, some were solid thunks, and some were very light and brisk. Then I opened my eyes and watched how everyone's feet struck the floor, and what sounds were made when they did.

I squeezed Paige's hand back. 'Thanks,' I said to her.

Still, as the line rolled round to me, I felt the pressure to get it right building. It was like waiting to be pelted in the face with rotten fruit.

Don't think about it too much, I repeated silently to myself. *Just do it, and see what happens.*

My turn.

Two sounds, my mind chanted. *A wing is two sounds. Out in, out in, scrape tap, scrape tap; out in, out in, scrape tap, scrape tap.*

Over and over in my head I said it until eventually my feet came into rhythm with my words, and I was doing it without thinking. No, the sound wasn't as crisp as Paige's steps, which came right after mine, but they were still there!

I began to feel that, maybe, this wouldn't be so impossible after all.

My feelings and confidence got stronger when we had to do shuffle-toe-heel turns across the room. I caught sight of myself in the mirror, turning and tapping like I'd been doing it for ages. My imagination put a top hat on my head, shiny black tap shoes with pink bows on my feet, and a tailcoat costume that glittered and caught the light as I spun.

I could do it. Tonight I would get Mum to ring the number on the flyer and book me an audition. And if I didn't get in, at least I'd know I tried.

But I *really* wanted to get in. And not just in the chorus. The starring role! I wanted to be Jane, who is one of the children Mary Poppins comes to look after.

I was so busy dreaming about this that I came out of a turn and ran into the girl in front of me.

'Sorry, Violet,' I muttered.

'That's what you spot for,' sassed Violet, but before I could give her a lashing of the Ellie attitude, Paige appeared at my side. Her blonde curls, angelic face and baby-powder smell straight away calmed me down.

'Killing it.' Paige grinned at me. 'Who knows, maybe one day we'll be doing tap duos together?'

'Maybe.' I laughed.

But in my mind, I was already beyond tap duos. I was the tapping queen of Broadway.

Only an audition stood in my way.

Chapter Six

Nibble, nibble, nibble.

Stop that.

A big chip of nail polish came off my nails, which I'd painted pink especially for the occasion.

The occasion being the audition, of course.

I'd booked it!

And now I was here!

I'd filled out my form and handed it in. (I may have lied about how much experience I had, but who doesn't? You don't get a leading role by being a nobody.) Now I was waiting for the group audition, where we would learn a short tap sequence and a musical theatre number, which we would then perform for the director and the two choreographers of the shows (Billie and the tap teacher).

The auditions were being held at a function centre in the city, but the actual rehearsals would be held at Silver Shoes. I took that as a good omen. To make myself feel less nervous, I imagined I really was going to audition for a big Broadway show in the 1920s.

There I went, walking down an alley to the building's side entrance, in a coat with a fur collar and a pretty hat with my pin curls poking out. When the porter held the door open for me I would say, 'Why, thank you, sir' and 'Oh golly, well, I never' and give him a sweet look with my big long lashes that fluttered like butterfly kisses whenever I blinked or closed my eyes.

My legs were starting to twitch nervously, so I got out of my seat and walked around the foyer, checking everyone out. Kids younger than me were there, as well as adults as old as my grandpa.

Most of them chatted to each other and seemed very comfortable. I told myself not to be scared, but I didn't see anyone I knew, except for a couple of faces I recognised from competitions. Oh, and Violet from tap class. But I sure wasn't going to talk to her.

Plus, I wanted to be by myself. To prepare. I could see people warming up and going through tap steps, but I felt very out of place and unlike my confident self at Silver Shoes.

I found a corridor running off the foyer and made sure it was empty. Then I shuffled my feet, going through tap steps that I thought might be used in the audition. I wanted it fresh in my memory.

'Beauuu-tiful mooorrrr-orrrr-orrrr-orrrr-orniiiiing,' came a voice from around the corner.

I poked my head around the wall to see who was singing.

It was a girl about my age, with fabulous burgundy-coloured hair, a small pointed nose and a large red mouth.

Well, maybe her mouth only looked large because she was singing in a very exaggerated way.

'Oh, hello,' she said. 'Sorry, did I disturb you? I'm just warming up.'

'No, that's okay,' I said.

'My name's Cadence Kohdean.' She flashed me a big smile that took up most of her face.

'Ellie,' I said, backing away from her teeth.

'I know the singing isn't till after,' Cadence explained, 'but vocal warm-ups help me get in the audition zone.'

'You have a nice voice,' I said, although my mind secretly added, *but mine is better.*

'Gosh, thank you,' said Cadence. 'I've been singing since I was two. This will be the third main role I've auditioned for. Last year I played the lead character in *Annie* and one of the von Trapp children in *The Sound of Music.* What parts have you played?'

'Um . . .' I fumbled, pushing my long ponytail off my shoulder. I couldn't make up something quick enough. 'I played Ariel in *The Little Mermaid*,' I finally said, which was a lie, unless you count a ten-minute performance of 'Under the Sea' in kindergarten. 'Usually I just go for the chorus. You get to do all the cool dances that way. Dancing is really my thing.'

'Yes! You totally look like a dancer,' said Cadence, in a tone of voice that made it hard to tell if she was giving me a compliment or not. 'I'm more of a singer. I've sung in front of the Prime Minister with the Youth Voices Choir, and also I've sung on a children's education CD. It was to learn your times tables.'

'You must be busy,' I said, taking another step away, because she had come right up to me. 'So you're going for the part of Jane?'

'Oh yes,' said Cadence. 'I think it will be great for my repertoire.'

I wasn't really sure what a repertoire was, but I knew straight away that this Cadence Kohdean was my main competition.

You can beat her, Ellie, I said to myself, but suddenly I really wanted Paige and Riley and Ash here with me. I always felt one hundred times more confident when they were around.

The stage manager called out that they were ready to begin the auditions, and for everyone to make their way to the stage.

'Here we go,' sang Cadence, with a dazzly little tap step that my eyes couldn't even keep up with, much less my feet. 'Good luck!'

'Thanks,' I said, following after her swinging ponytail. 'You too.'

But I wasn't sure if I meant it.

Chapter Seven

Snakes, spiders, sand in your bathers, being dobbed on for something that wasn't your fault, maths tests, jelly snakes not coming in pink. All these things are horrible, but none give me the throat-swelling, stomach-clenching, shaky fingers and brain-muddling that auditions do.

The only person I know who hates auditions more than me is Paige. I just don't think it's fair that everything you've worked and studied for can come down to a five-minute audition. I bet if I had to hand in a video montage of all my best performances instead of doing an audition, I would get the part each time.

For the *Mary Poppins* auditions, we started off learning the jazz-based musical theatre dance, which Billie was in charge of. Having Billie there made me feel a little more at home and took some of the tightness out of my shoulders.

She began by getting us to do some floor work: turns, kicks, travelling steps. I had to smother a giggle when the adults tried some of them. I've seen better performances from an emu.

Next, Billie taught us a routine so that she could get an idea of everyone's dance ability.

The choreography was fairly simple with a four-count beat. I could have done it in my sleep, but I still made sure I was at the front, and on my best Ellie-is-a-good-student behaviour. Because I found the routine so easy I tried to up my energy and flair. The simplicity of the dance sequence also gave me a good chance to watch everyone else and suss out the competition, especially Cadence. Sure, she got all the steps, but she wasn't *that* great.

Billie let the adults sit down after that, because next she had choreographed a piece to teach the kids who wanted to be in the main dance troupe. The adults who didn't get a main part would be in the chorus, singing and doing all the background stuff, while the main dance troupe would be front and centre, doing the bulk of the choreography.

This musical theatre routine was more complicated, with some turns and jumps and showy steps. I nailed it, of course, and I felt a beam of pride when I saw Cadence watching me.

Billie also got us to do a short contemporary sequence.

'*Mary Poppins* has room for many styles of dance,' she called out after we were all done and standing around with our hands on our knees, catching our breaths. 'So we'll be doing some jazzy, musical-theatre based pieces, as well as more lyrical pieces to the slower songs. And then, of course, good ol' tap.'

At this a lot of people cheered, and I felt my stomach sink. I casually moved back to the second row so I would have someone to copy from if worse came to worst, even if that someone was Cadence, who I noticed pushed her way to the front almost immediately.

Billie made a fake sad face and clutched her chest. 'And this is where I will now leave you, my lovelies – and pass the baton to tap extraordinaire Damon Periwinkle.'

Damon *who*? I covered my laugh with my hand and looked around to see if anyone else found it funny. No one. They were all staring at Mr Periwinkle with pleasant faces. I rolled my eyes. Ash, Riley and Paige would have shared my secret smile.

Periwinkle jumped to his feet when Billie called out his name. He was at least sixty, with long lanky legs, but he moved with so much grace, effortlessly jumping over some chairs that were in his way, swinging himself around a pot plant, and tapping his way to the front.

He had thick black hair brushed back neatly and the darkest, twinkliest eyes turned up at the edges with crinkles. His mouth looked as if he was always in the middle of sharing a joke with you.

Despite his silly name, I liked him straight away. He reminded me of an old movie star, and I imagined that when he was on stage you couldn't take your eyes off him.

'Welcome, my hoofers,' he said with a very British accent, bowing to us theatrically. 'I've been watching all of you dance your little hearts out. Now it's time for you to watch me. Who wants to do some tapping?'

'Me!' trilled Cadence.

'Not me!' I muttered under my breath.

'Who said "not me"?' Periwinkle asked, whirling around and searching us all with mock anger.

I tried to stare pointedly at Cadence to make it seem like she'd said it, but I could feel my face going red. I had to call on all my acting training to not give myself away.

'Well, whoever said that, I'll make you regret it,' Periwinkle teased. 'What's the first rule of Broadway?'

'Always be ready,' Cadence said.

'You got it, honey,' he said with a wink. 'Let's tap.'

Never in my life had I heard that 'Always Be Ready' was the first rule of Broadway. Cadence probably paid him five dollars so he could say that and she would answer to look good.

I set my jaw. Too bad, Cadence Kohdean. It took more than that to put me off.

Chapter Eight

The first thing I noticed was that although Cadence had been just okay in the other dances, tap was obviously her style. Every sound she made was crisp and clean, and all her movements expressive. She seemed to know what tap step we were going to do, even before Periwinkle had shown it to us.

I kept my competition antennae out. There were some good tappers, but I knew by far

I'd been the best in the other dances. So the role of Jane could very well come down to me and Cadence. That's if she hadn't bribed the director, too.

No! I would fight for the part of Jane. I focused on Periwinkle's feet, mimicking his every ball dig, back brush and ball change.

He started teaching us a short routine. His style of tap was very fluid – it wasn't the straight-spine-arms-do-very-little kind of tap. Instead, all the tap steps flowed into beautiful body shapes and energetic kicks or jumps, taking up every inch of available floor space.

I took a lot of joy in trying to copy Periwinkle's athletic moves and the feeling of lightness his body created. My feet let me down a little when it came to catching and hitting all the tap sounds. A few times I just made something up and hoped it sounded okay because the feet totally lost me.

Cadence, of course, didn't put one shiny black tap wrong. But I didn't mind. I felt a sense of achievement that a week ago I hadn't tapped properly since I was a tiny, and now I'd just successfully completed a tap audition. The idea that I could make music with my feet was a bit of a thrill!

But I still had the singing audition tomorrow. One more test to pass before I was crowned an official triple threat.

***

I was feeling quite good when I walked into the foyer the next day, ready to sing my heart out.

Ugh.

You'll never guess who was waiting before me.

Cadence Kohdean.

Today her long burgundy hair was pulled into two braids and she was wearing a pretty white smock dress with little black booties. She looked like Jane without even trying. I was just wearing my favourite pink floaty top and my good luck silver leggings.

'Oh hey!' she said. 'Ellie, right?'

'Right,' I said.

'I must be auditioning before you,' said Cadence, like it wasn't already obvious. 'How exciting! What are you singing?'

'"The Perfect Nanny",' I said, naming a song from *Mary Poppins*.

'Oh, that's nice,' said Cadence. 'I'm doing "Green Finch and Linnet Bird" from *Sweeney Todd*. I feel it really shows my range. Plus it's not always a good idea to do a song from the show you're actually auditioning for.' She smiled at me. 'But I'm sure they won't mind.'

'I know that,' I lied, sweeping imaginary dust off the sleeve of my top. 'I'm just being proactive. That way I can really express the character of Jane while I'm singing her song.'

'Oh, absolutely,' said Cadence, who got up as soon as I sat next to her on the couch. 'Excuse me, it's almost my turn. I'm just going to do some warming up.'

'I did it at home,' I lied again.

'Oh, whoops,' she said, turning back to pick up a bottle from the couch. 'Pineapple juice. It helps smooth out your throat.' She took a delicate sip, and then started to walk back and forth across the room, sirening.

As I've recently found out from my singing classes, sirening is where you try to make a sound in your throat that goes up and down, kind of like an actual siren. Then she sang phrases like 'red leather, yellow leather', and 'one, one two one, one two three two one', switching her register.

For such an annoying know-it-all, she sure had a pretty voice. It was sweet and clear. My voice was powerful, but it was much deeper than Cadence's. I bet when Cadence was a baby she didn't even have a first word, she just had a first note.

I knew I should get up and warm-up too, but I felt self-conscious. Instead I brought out the script I had to read Jane's part from and studied it without much going into my head at all.

The door to the next room opened and a boy came out, very red in the face.

'Hey there,' said Cadence, as he went down the stairs. 'How did you go?'

'They make you do a British accent,' the boy groaned. 'Mine was so bad!'

'Oh well,' said Cadence cheerily. 'It's not over till it's over.'

'Yeah,' said the boy, putting his cap back on his head. 'Thanks. See ya.'

Cadence waved daintily at him while I shifted uncomfortably in my seat. I took a nervous sip of my water. Straight away I needed to pee.

The door to the auditorium opened again and the stage manager poked her head out. 'Cadence Kohdean?' she asked.

'Right here,' trilled Cadence. 'Hello!'

'You're next, sweetheart.' The stage manager beamed at her.

'Perfect.' Cadence beamed back.

'Perfect,' I grumbled to myself, and then switched to a smile as Cadence turned to me.

'Well, this is it!' she said. 'Good luck, Ellie! Hopefully I'll see you at rehearsals.'

'Hopefully,' I said back, wanting to tip the pineapple juice all over her dress.

But there was only one way I would ever want to see her at rehearsals. And that's if I was playing Jane.

Chapter Nine

After Cadence had skipped into the room like nervousness was allergic to her, I got up off the couch. The air smelled like her cherry blossom perfume. I took out my strawberry vanilla body spray (my signature scent) and used it to remove all traces of her.

I walked around the foyer, humming to myself.

I went to the toilet, where I found out I didn't need to pee after all.

When I came back I could hear Cadence singing. She could have made the rotten fruit in the bottom of our fridge turn ripe again. Her voice must have been made out of sugar and candied flowers.

Perfect Cadence Kohdean. My biggest rival for Jane. And the worst thing was she was much harder to hate than, say, Jasmine. Cadence was never outwardly snotty to me; she was always nice and happy and super talented.

I kept doing my slow hums and sipping my water, but really I was listening to Cadence sing and then read off the script in a British accent so perfect it was like she'd been born there.

I almost freaked myself out but then I remembered Paige's voice saying, 'She's good but you're good too, Ellie. In a different way.

It just comes down to who's the best fit for the role. Don't be so hard on yourself. This is your first musical theatre audition. Just to get in the chorus is great.'

So I took a big breath, straightened my tights and told myself that even if I didn't feel confident I had to act like I was, because *my* first rule of showbiz was to fake it till you make it.

So I beamed as brightly at Cadence as she did at me when she came out of her audition, and when I walked into the room for my turn, I covered the beating of my heart with a big smile.

'Hello again,' said the director. 'Welcome. Ellie, isn't it?'

'Yes, it is,' I said, imagining Cadence. 'Pleased to meet you.'

Billie and Periwinkle were seated on one side of the director, while the musical director,

Stella, and someone else I didn't know, were on his other. They all stared at me, pinning me like a bug in the too-bright room. I focused on Billie and her encouraging smile. I knew she wanted me to do well and it gave me confidence.

'We were very impressed with your dancing yesterday,' said the director.

'Thank you,' I said. 'I love dancing. It's my favourite thing in the world.'

'Lovely.' The director joined his hands together. 'Let's have a listen to your singing then, shall we? What will you be performing for us today?'

'"The Perfect Nanny,"' I pronounced clearly, and went over and gave my sheet music to the old man at the piano. He gave me a friendly nod that also made my heart settle a bit.

'Well,' said the director, 'show us your stuff.'

Oh, I'll show you.

And I opened my mouth and began to sing.

***

'So,' I whispered to Riley, as I arched over my crossed knees, 'I started off on the wrong note, and then I forgot one of the words so my timing was off. It was pretty awful, but I quickly recovered and absolutely belted out the rest. I even reached the high note I've been having trouble with.'

'Yay, Ellie!' said Paige on my other side, as we switched to our backs and prepared to do leg kicks. 'I bet you impressed the director!'

I tucked my left foot up so the sole was on the floor and began to kick up and down with my right.

'Point, flex, lower down,' Miss Caroline called out from the front of the class.

'Well, they didn't boo me out of the room,' I said, 'so I guess that's a good start. Also, Billie gave me a sneaky high five as I left.

That's gotta mean she was happy with me, right?'

'What?' hissed Ashley, on the other side of Riley. 'What did you say? That Billie got *eaten alive*?'

Riley snorted down her laughter. 'Get your ears cleaned out, Ash,' she said, affectionately.

'But I'm all the way over here!' Ashley whispered. 'I need a telephone just to speak to you.'

'Can you be quiet!' Jasmine hissed, turning around to glare at us. 'Some of us are trying to stretch.' She rolled her eyes at Tove.

'Oh, don't worry, Jasmine,' said Ashley. 'It doesn't matter how hard you stretch your face, it won't improve.'

'Sorry, I left my laughter at home,' Jasmine threw over her shoulder.

'Shhhh,' said Riley. 'Will you keep it down? I'm trying to stretch.'

'Everyone, hush!' Miss Caroline called. 'I can hear whispering back there. Any more and I'll make you do a double set of ab work.'

'Good,' joked Ashley. 'I ate too much Chinese last night.'

'Oh, food,' I sighed, kicking a leg over my head. 'I could really go some jelly snakes right about now.'

'I have a fresh packet in my bag,' Paige whispered. 'I got the sour ones. You know, with the strawberry flavour.'

'If I wanted sour snakes, I could just wipe them on Jasmine's face,' I said.

'Ellie!' scolded Paige, who doesn't like being nasty to anyone.

'It's not mean if it's the truth,' I whispered back.

I stopped talking then, because we had to do crunches and ab exercises. A lot of people don't understand why we spend so much time on them in class, but when it comes to dancing you have to use your whole body. So the stronger and more stable your core, the more balance and strength you'll have.

I tried to focus all the way through jazz class, but I was worried about the audition. What if I hadn't done enough to get in? What if I didn't even get into the chorus?

I didn't know how I would be able to bear the wait until I found out.

Chapter Ten

At the end of class, and after many snakes had
been devoured, I slung my dance bag over my
shoulder and trudged down the steps of Silver
Shoes to go home.

'Ellie!' my little brother, Lucas, squealed.
He scrambled off from where he was playing
on the monkey bars and flung himself towards
me, giggling. 'A somersault, Ellie,' he squealed.
'I did a somersault from the monkeys!'

'That's so brave!' I said, picking him up and giving him a cuddle. It instantly made me feel better, like it always does. 'Did you get dizzy?' I asked him.

'Not me!' he said, and then he caught sight of Paige and wriggled out of my arms.

'Paige, Paige!' he yelled. 'I did a somersault from the monkeys!'

While Paige fussed over him (she doesn't have any brothers or sisters, so I think she really loves spending time with Lucas), I dumped all my stuff in the car, which Mum had parked out the front.

'Hey honey,' she said.

'Hey.' I took a big swig from my water bottle.

'Guess who I got a call from today,' Mum said.

'Um, Nan?' I said, swallowing my water and taking another big gulp.

'Hmm,' said Mum. 'Do you happen to know a director of the musical *Mary Poppins*?'

I stopped drinking and stared at Mum, water dribbling down the sides of my mouth.

'That's one of your best looks, sweetie,' Mum teased.

I wiped my mouth with the back of my hand. 'And?' I asked, almost too scared to hear the answer. My stomach cramped up and my skin got all hot.

'And,' Mum said, with a sneaky smile, 'she might have said something about welcoming you to the main dance chorus of *Mary Poppins*!'

I stared at her.

'Congratulations, honey!' she said.

'The chorus?' I repeated. 'She didn't say anything about Jane?'

'No,' said Mum. 'But you got in, Ellie! On your first try. You should be proud!'

'Who got Jane then?' I asked. 'Did she say?'

Mum frowned at me and put one hand on her hip. 'We had a good chat, actually,' she said, watching me very carefully. 'Turns out I know the director from the gym. She was telling me all about the sho–'

'Mum,' I interrupted. 'Did she say who got Jane?'

'Yes,' said Mum.

'And?'

'Cadence Kohdean.'

I felt my musical theatre career crashing down around me. All my nightmares had come true. Paige chose that moment to walk up with Lucas hanging off her hand.

'Hi Mrs Irvin,' she said. 'How are you doing?'

'I'm doing very well,' said Mum. 'As should Ellie, here. She got into the chorus of *Mary Poppins*!'

'Oh, Ellie!' Paige said, rushing to give me a hug. 'That's so amazing. Well done! You'll get to do so much cool dancing in the chorus!'

'Don't, Paige.' I pushed her away. 'What would you know about it?'

'Ellie,' warned Mum.

Lucas took a tiny step away from all of us.

I sighed. 'Sorry,' I said. 'I just really wanted to get Jane.'

'That's okay,' said Paige, very quietly.

'It isn't,' said Mum, turning to me. 'It was very rude.'

'I said I was sorry!' I yelled.

Mum gave me a look that said I should get in the car quick-smart or there would be trouble.

'Sorry again,' I said to Paige. 'See you tomorrow at school.'

She gave me a small wave. I felt bad about snapping at her.

But I felt even worse that Cadence had beaten me.

Chapter Eleven

It took me a few days to get over that I'd lost out to Cadence, but by the time our first rehearsal for *Mary Poppins* rolled around I was feeling a little more excited.

Rehearsals for the show were held on Tuesday nights and Sunday during the day. That was as well as having jazz on Wednesdays, technique class on Thursdays, and lyrical on Saturday mornings.

'I'm not made of petrol,' Mum grumbled, as she drove me to Silver Shoes.

'When I'm rich and famous, Mum,' I told her, 'and the biggest star on Broadway, I'll have a personal assistant to drive me everywhere – and probably you, too.'

'Right,' said Mum. 'Because it's so hard right now to walk the five minutes to work.'

But I saw that she was smothering a smile and really quite liked the idea of having a world-famous daughter.

On Tuesdays we worked on songs while Sundays were dedicated to dance and acting. I quickly got used to seeing people carrying around pineapple juice, but when I got Mum to buy me some, it made my throat feel all warm and thick. I kept drinking it, though. I wanted to fit in.

Speaking of fitting in, I was finding it a bit hard.

At Silver Shoes I was used to walking in and having everyone not only being the same age as me, but knowing who I was. Sometimes they even looked up to me, like if they didn't know a step and wanted me to show them.

But with *Mary Poppins* I felt like no one cared about me at all, and I had nothing in common with them. Plus, they all liked to quote songs from musicals and had weird musical theatre in-jokes that I didn't understand. So I felt a bit left out.

It was very, very different from Silver Shoes.

But when Mum dropped me off, once again I told myself to just go for it. And so I walked into the studio with my performance face firmly in place.

The first song we had to learn was called 'Step in Time'.

'Okay!' said Stella, the musical director, clapping her hands to get our attention (that's because everyone was talking, except for me, sitting in the corner like Nelly No-Friends).

'This is our big showstopper for Act Two! We'll have some tap with our main dance troupe, some jazz from everyone else, and we'll have the leads on as well. So we need big voices and even bigger energy. Cadence, would you like to hand these out, and can I have all the children on this side of the room and the adults on the other.'

Cadence skipped around giving everyone the sheet music.

'Here you go, Ellie.' She smiled as I took the stapled sheets from her dainty little hands.

As soon as I looked at the notes in front of me my head exploded. I'd only just begun my singing lessons, so I was used to simple sheet music with minimal notes.

But this sheet had four different lines of music just for one lyric, with everyone's different parts, and so many squiggles that I could barely tell what was a minim and what was a semibreve.

Cadence must have seen my face because she stopped in front of me and laid her hand on my arm. 'Don't worry, Ellie,' she said. 'It will all make sense soon enough.'

I quickly plastered on my best Silver Shoes showgirl face. 'Oh, it makes sense right now,' I said, channelling Paige and her sweet tones. 'I'm just worried about some of these high notes. They'll be hard for other people to hit. Not me, because I'm a mezzo-soprano.'

I was hoping with all my might that I'd used the term 'mezzo-soprano' right. I wasn't really one of those – in fact, I didn't really know what I was. I just remembered the term from a sheet on vocal ranges that Billie had given me when I first started my singing lessons.

But I must have used it right because

Cadence's whole face shone. 'Me too!' she said. 'Singing sisters!' She opened her mouth and out came the most ridiculous high-pitched sound that was so angelic it made my voice sound like a gargoyle's.

Lucky I was saved from having to show off my own range, because Stella got the pianist to start. I shook out my pages and pretended that I was still at Silver Shoes and knew exactly what I was doing.

Good thing I was a terrific actress. I hadn't gotten into *Mary Poppins* for nothing!

I would fake it and keep my eyes and ears open, and learn. We'd see who would be breaking the windows with their mezzo-soprano then.

Chapter Twelve

I sat in the corner of the rehearsal space feeling very un-Ellie like.

All around me people were sitting in groups, chatting and sharing the lunches they'd packed for rehearsal break.

And here I was, eating my lunch all alone, after a morning of being told off because I kept missing the downbeats in my tapping, and getting so flustered over trying to get it right that I felt my head was about to fall off.

I was meant to be making an impression! This was my big break, my first musical theatre experience! In my dreams I'd always wowed people with my talent, this girl who'd come out of nowhere and won everyone's hearts.

But some of the cast didn't even know me. Today, one of the adults had asked me to move up and said, 'Sorry, what's your name again, sweetie?'

What? *Everyone* knows my name is Eleanor Irvin. Even the juniors at Silver Shoes, even their parents! I have a whole shelf full of trophies and medals from talent shows, competitions, exams and eisteddfods. And this adult was asking me to *move up*?

I shuffled over on the bench to where a group of kids were sitting on the floor, eating cake one of them had brought in.

I wrinkled my nose. Coconut. Me and the Silver Shoes girls always had caramel and Jamaican apple – Riley's mum made the best cake you've ever tasted.

'Remember when we were at music camp,' one of them was saying. The others nodded so I nodded too, although I'd never been to a music camp in all my life. 'And we did that tribute to *Little Shop of Horrors* but Macey's flower mask was so big and she couldn't see where she was going?'

The others burst out laughing. I went to smile but all that went up was my eyebrows. I sighed.

Jelly snakes were the only things that would save me now. I dug some out of my bag and carried them outside.

There was a garden near where Lucas had been playing on the monkey bars. It was bricked in and had overgrown bushes and twisty paths, and I followed them until I found a park bench under a eucalyptus tree.

I undid the tie around the snakes packet. Inside was a folded-up piece of paper. I smoothed it out and found something written inside:

We miss you, Broadway Baby! Have fun at rehearsals! Love P, R & A

They must have snuck it in there at Silver Shoes when I hadn't noticed.

I held the note in my hand and struggled not to cry. If only *Mary Poppins* had an Ashley, or a Riley, or a Paige, it would be ten times more fun.

A sherbet bomb dropped onto my head.

'Huh?' I stared at it lying in my lap. A girly giggle floated down from the leaves above me.

I looked up.

Cadence Kohdean was sitting up in the branches. You couldn't have surprised me more if Jasmine had opened her mouth and said something nice.

'Hello!' said Cadence.

'Hi,' I managed to say.

'Do you like climbing trees, Ellie?' asked Cadence. She slithered down the trunk with more skill than her perfect clothes and pretty little hands suggested.

'It's okay,' I said. 'Not really my number one hobby. I wouldn't have thought it was yours, either.'

'Four brothers.' Cadence giggled again, seating herself next to me. 'They also taught me how to fart in my armpit!' She clutched at my arm. 'Don't tell anyone, though.'

'Um,' I said, 'it's not really how I would start a conversation.'

Not that I've managed to start one at all, anyway.

'Oooh!' Cadence squealed when she saw what was on my lap. 'You've got snakes! Want to swap? Snakes are my next favourite after sherbet bombs.' She waved the packet in front of my face.

'Sure,' I said, offering her mine. 'The pink ones are the best. Not many companies make them.'

Cadence happily helped herself to my snakes.

'Thought you'd be more of a lollipop girl,' I said.

'Well, Ellie,' said Cadence, her eyes sparkling, 'there's probably a lot of things you don't know about me.'

I looked down. 'Probably,' I said, trying not to picture Mum shaking her head at me and saying, 'Don't judge a book by its cover'. I guess I was a little guilty of that.

Cadence playfully hit me with a snake. 'I know they're all totally crazy about musical theatre,' she said, 'but sometimes I just want to talk about pop music, you know? I mean, Taylor Swift's new song . . .'

'I love Taylor Swift!' I blurted.

Cadence clapped her hands and started singing 'Shake it Off' and I joined in. Our voices worked together quite well.

I guess you can say that's how I ended up finding out that Cadence Kohdean wasn't so bad after all.

Chapter Thirteen

'Girls!' I yelled, barrelling into technique class.

Ashley, Riley and Paige turned around like I was a bowling ball and they were the pins I was about to strike.

I flung myself at them and we all tumbled to the ground in a big heap.

'Ellie!' Paige protested, wriggling her way out from under a pile of salmon-coloured legs (technique tights are the worst). 'Hey, you didn't come round after school yesterday. Remember we were going to make candles?'

'Sorry,' I said. 'I completely forgot. I went to the music store with Cadence.'

Paige frowned. 'Oh. I thought you didn't like her.'

'She's okay.' I shrugged. 'I miss you guys, though! *Mary Poppins* isn't the same without my girls!' I ruffled Ashley's hair. Her bangs were already falling out of her bun.

'Ellie, how many jelly snakes have you had?' she asked, trying to tidy up her fringe.

'Here,' said Paige, reaching to twist Ashley's hair back. 'I've got a spare bobby pin.'

'Ugh,' said Ashley. 'My hair eats those like they're jelly snakes.'

'That's why you do the braids, darling,' said Riley in a fake posh voice, modelling the two, tight braids she always wears. 'No bobby pins needed.'

'Ugh,' said Jasmine, who just so happened to walk by then with Tove, as always, half a step behind her. 'Look, Tove, a pile of rubbish on the floor.'

'Jasmine!' gasped Ashley, jumping up in horror. 'I'm so sorry! I heard you lost your personality but I didn't believe the rumours until now!'

Riley smirked but Paige, who hates fighting, looked down.

I didn't really feel like adding onto Ashley's quip, although normally I would have. I thought, maybe, having spent the past couple of weeks being an outcast at *Mary Poppins*, that I understood a bit about what it was like to feel ganged up on. Also I thought maybe I had a better idea of why Jasmine was the way she was.

Sometimes it's better to be defensive than vulnerable.

Miss Caroline clapped then to begin the class. I fell into the familiar rhythm of doing warm-ups that I'd done a million times before: flex and point, isolations, body rolls, leg kicks, tendus, splits. I was good at these things because I knew how to do them – I approached them with a confident attitude.

Was that my problem at *Mary Poppins*? Maybe I wasn't faking it till I was making it well enough and I needed to build up my confidence, because I'd definitely never lacked that before.

Or maybe I had to believe I was right where I needed to be and deserved to be there as much as anyone else. It had just been such a long time since I'd really, really had to work at being the best, instead of it being natural. And if I didn't get over myself and push myself, confidently, then I would never improve.

We practised our turns next – first preps, then single turns, then double.

'Go for the triple if you like,' Miss Caroline called out. 'Strong supporting leg, core engaged, arms sharp and shooting out or the momentum won't take you round. Spot, spot, spot!'

Then we divided into two groups to do travelling turns across the floor – port de bras single, port de bras double, port de bras triple.

I decided to put my thoughts into action.

Triple turns. I'd never managed to success-fully complete a full one. But today was my day.

I psyched myself up while Miss Caroline counted us in. Off Paige and I went. *One two three, prepare, turn.* No problems there. *One two three, prepare, double turn.* Paige fell out of it but BAM! my feet and face landed dead on. Paige stopped then but I barely noticed.

My gaze was set straight ahead. Focus.

Port de bras, prepare. Turn one . . . two . . . focus, Ellie, do everything that Miss Caroline said you should, don't give up halfway through, push through, want it, know you can do it . . . three!

My feet came together, I was facing the right way, and I wasn't sprawled on my bum.

My first triple turn!

I heard Riley and Ash cheering from the corner.

I knew, then. It may have been just a triple turn, but it was like I found the old Ellie somewhere in the middle of spinning and hurled her back into the world.

And boy, was she glad to be back!

Chapter Fourteen

One chassé, chaîné, gallop, jeté! Perfect!

One tuck jump, step through, arabesque. Beautiful!

Turn, turn, turn, and split jump. Got it!

'Yes!' Billie called, jumping down from the stage where she was sitting. 'Nailed it! My head just exploded from the greatness! Go have some water, my honeys! I love you all!'

I went to retrieve my pink drink bottle with a spring in my step. My confidence from class at Silver Shoes had carried into my *Mary Poppins* rehearsal. I walked into it with a 'positive mind', and once my head was clear of being uncomfortable and shy, it was so much easier to believe in my ability to dance.

'Ellie, you're such a good dancer,' Cadence sighed as I took a big swig from my water (Mum had added orange slices and berries in the bottom, and it was all kinds of delicious). 'I was meant to be here learning my lines for Act One Scene Two,' she continued, 'but instead I've been watching you. The height you got on that jeté! I can only get that high in my dreams.'

'Well, Cadence,' I said, 'your mind and heart can take you places even your body didn't think you could go.'

I don't know where that came from, but I decided it made me sound really smart so I just shrugged and took another swig of water as if I said wise things like that all the time.

'You're going to be so famous, Ellie,' said Cadence. 'It will be, like, one minute you're here and the next you've got your own headlining show on Broadway.'

'Fabulous!' I said, pulling out my packet of snakes and offering them to her. 'I'll still be able to see you, because you'll have the starring role in *Cats* or *Chicago* or something.'

'Cadence Kohdean and Eleanor Irvin, the "It" girls.' Cadence giggled. 'From the back streets of Bayside to the bright lights of Broadway!' She pulled out a handful of snakes and wrinkled her nose. 'Gosh,' she said, 'I so wish they would make these in pink.'

'Yes!' I exclaimed. 'Cadence, are you me in another body?'

'I hope so,' said Cadence, 'because I want to wear this!' She touched the fluoro crop top and short set I was wearing (a bargain from the Dance Ahoy online shop, which I'd sneakily looked at when I was banned from the internet, and then convinced Mum to buy).

After we were well gorged on snakes, sherbet bombs and the butterfly cupcakes Cadence's mum had packed her, we moved on to the tap sequence for the main number in Act Two, 'Step in Time', which we'd learnt to sing the other day.

I didn't let any negative thoughts come into my head, and I went straight to the front of the group (still at the side, though, so I could watch others if I needed to). There would be no more hiding in the back for me!

The dance started off easy and slow before building up to a bang, when the notes spilled out like they couldn't hold back any longer. The choreography was basic toe punches and slaps and stomps to begin with, just punctuating the music. Easy enough, but I made sure my tapping was crisp and sharp, and that my rhythm was worthy of Gene Kelly. (Just in case you don't know, Gene Kelly is a famous movie-star tapper. I know, because I'd spent three hours looking him up on YouTube last night. Oh yeah, while still being banned. But education waits for no one).

Things quickly got more complicated though, but I stayed cool.

Don't think about it too much. Just watch Periwinkle's feet, listen to the rhythm of his taps, and let your feet move how they naturally move to copy the sound.

So when we had to do a time step, which involves brushes and shuffles and a transfer of weight on the feet, at first glance my mind went 'eek!', but then I broke it down and trusted my feet and suddenly I was doing the move like my name was Cadence Kohdean. My feet were making music!

I felt like I'd broken through a barrier. Tap was quickly becoming one of my favourite styles of dance, although I would never turn my back on my beloved jazz.

Billie, Periwinkle and the director asked to speak with me at the end of the day. Wham. I felt a force field of worry hit me. Was I fooling myself? Had I just made a joke out of my dancing? Were they going to tell me I wasn't quite up to being in the musical?

'Ellie, dear Ellie,' said Periwinkle after rehearsal.

'Yes?' I gulped.

'We've been keeping a close eye on all the dancers,' said Periwinkle. 'Especially today, because there are minor roles in some of the dances and scenes we haven't filled yet.'

'It will mainly be dancing parts,' Billie said, smiling.

'Yes,' said the director. 'There's a doll in "Playing the Game", a statue that comes to life in "Jolly Holiday", and a small singing part for a girl in "Let's Go Fly a Kite".'

I nodded. I'm sure my eyes were popping out of my head.

'You're quite the little dancer,' said Periwinkle. 'And Billie particularly sings your praises. You've got a very powerful voice, too.'

'Really?' I squeaked. 'Thank you.'

'There's no missing you,' joked the director. 'So we'd like to give these few small roles to you. We can see you'd do a great job and are very dedicated.'

My heart stopped. My breath was caught. I risked a look at Billie, who was wearing the proudest, silliest grin. I felt my own mouth start to split in half.

It wasn't quite the part of Jane. But it was a good start.

'I'd love to!' I exclaimed.

Chapter Fifteen

Well, as if my busy schedule wasn't enough! At the next rehearsal the director had announced that the Bayside council was holding a fundraising variety night and the cast of *Mary Poppins* were going to perform a number from the upcoming show.

'A small taste of what's to come,' Periwinkle had added. 'But not enough to give everything away. Leave 'em wanting more.'

It was very exciting, of course. Any chance to perform on stage gets my blood pumping. But it also meant that we only had a couple of weeks to put together a number for the variety night.

Extra rehearsals were called.

"The number Billie and I have decided to do, in consultation with the director –' Periwinkle flashed an oily smile her way that made me think he didn't really like her (only 'cause I've flashed the same smile myself sometimes) '– is the number we've been working on, "Step In Time". It's the big musical piece of the show. We need the main cast, the chorus of tap dancers, and everyone else for the jazz movement in the background. It's a very long song, so we'll only do about five minutes of it.'

'And I'm warning you now,' Billie cut in, 'that what I make up may change by the time it comes to the actual show run. I'm notorious for doing that.'

'What's notorious?' asked one of the girls (a great dancer but her singing wouldn't win her first place on *The Voice*, and I guess neither would her IQ). Cadence and I swapped an amused glance and it was almost like I was back with Ash, Riley and Paige at Silver Shoes.

Notorious, of course, means that you are well-known, not always in a positive way (ahem, not that I had to google it or anything).

As soon as I knew a performance was involved and I was going to be on stage and in my natural element, I felt the stage blood in my veins go fizzy. I had the beans; I couldn't wait to start.

First we had to get the singing out of the way – and I'm talking a whole morning of it. Lucky the song was catchy and had a lot of harmonies and dynamics, or I would have fallen asleep and dribbled all over Cadence's designer dance tights.

The song featured Bert the chimney sweep and Mary Poppins as the main singers, with Jane and her brother supporting them, and then the chorus joining in, either as chimney sweeps (the tap troupe) or villagers (the adults).

The song began with these piano chords that you knew were going to build up to something big. Bert sang first, and then the chorus joined in after him, before everyone launched into the next verse together.

I know it might sound simple, but when the chorus came in, with the younger voices of the chimney sweeps, and then the more adult voices rounding them out and softly coming in over them, it sounded like a gospel choir. Shivers ran up my spine. The mix of voices kept building, building, building, until I thought my heart would burst as it soared with the beautiful sound everyone made when they sang as one.

It really was like magic.

At lunch break Cadence and I were sitting on the steps out the front of the hall laughing about it. We talked over each other in our excitement, and tried to chuck pieces of snake into each other's mouths, all at the same time.

I was having so much fun with Cadence, I almost couldn't believe I once thought she'd been a prissy goody-goody.

That was when Riley and Paige came out from the side door of Silver Shoes and headed towards us.

Chapter Sixteen

'Hi Ellie,' said Paige, beaming my way. She paused a couple of steps in front of me, and Riley stopped a step or so behind her, in what I call her 'Riley' pose: standing back on one leg, arms crossed, sussing out the situation.

We usually have lyrical on Saturday mornings, you see, although Billie had pulled a few strings so I could miss it just while we were having these extra rehearsals.

'Hi guys,' I said. 'How was lyrical?'

Paige darted a quick look at Cadence, while Riley made it obvious she was checking Cadence out. Cadence, for her part, was smiling prettily and warmly, giving Paige a run for her money in the innocent department.

'We started the dance for "Say Something" today,' Paige said. 'But don't worry, I'll catch you up if you like.' She zipped another quick look at Cadence before she held out a packet of snakes. 'We brought you some snakes in case you were hungry.'

I looked down at the parade of snake parts on the steps, and the packet of sherbet bombs open between me and Cadence.

'Oh!' I said. 'Thanks, Paige, but I think we may have had enough sugar already!'

Cadence giggled.

'Right,' said Paige, folding up the packet

and taking a step back closer to Riley. 'That's okay. Maybe next time.'

'*I'll* have some,' said Riley, snatching the packet from Paige and making a point of choosing one. 'Thank you, Paige.' She chewed on a red snake and turned her eyes to Cadence. 'Hi,' she said. 'Who are you?'

Cadence jumped up. 'Hello!' She dashed forward to give a dainty hug to Riley (who almost choked on her snake) and then did the same to Paige (who flinched like Cadence had thrown the whole packet at her). 'I'm Cadence Kohdean, Ellie's friend from *Mary Poppins*. You must be . . . hmm . . . Paige and Riley! Ellie talks about you all the time! She just loves Silver Shoes.'

'We know,' Paige mumbled to the ground.

'Oh yes,' said Riley, 'Ellie talks about you all the time, too.' She smirked when she said that because mostly what I'd told her and Paige and Ash was how annoying Cadence was and how much I disliked her. Now, things had obviously changed, because here I was sitting on the steps talking and laughing and eating lollies with her almost as if she was a Silver Shoes girl herself.

I flashed Riley a warning look to let her know that it wasn't the right time to go causing trouble for me and Cadence. Riley just shrugged and selected another snake.

There was a horrible silence between us four, which my mouth did not like, so it immediately opened and started babbling.

'It's so fun, what we're doing,' I said.

'You should hear the song we're working on,' said Cadence.

'It's so catchy,' I hurried on. 'I wish we could do it in jazz, except a lot of it is tap – well, the part we're learning – well, me anyway, 'cause

I'm a chimney sweep. Cadence is playing Jane, that's the lead character.'

'I know who Jane is,' said Riley, although I wasn't sure she did.

'Oh! You're a fan of *Mary Poppins*?' said Cadence. 'Awesome! Ellie and I think it might be our favourite musical.'

Paige looked up at that, because she knew very well my favourite musical was *Hairspray* since I'd made her watch it with me a million times until it became hers, too. She caught my eye but then quickly looked down. She was holding her head in that way she does when she's trying not to get upset. It made my chest feel yucky. Of course *Hairspray* was my number one, but it's easy to get carried away when you're in the middle of doing another musical and having so much fun.

Another horrible silence.

'Are you guys going to come watch us at the preview performance for the variety night?' Cadence chirped. 'It will be super fun! You'll get to see what Ellie and I have been working on!'

'Can't wait,' said Riley.

'My mum's waiting to pick me up,' Paige said, miserably. She was clutching the bag of snakes so tight I thought they might combust. 'Bye, Ellie.' She walked away, looking like a fairy who'd just lost her wings.

'Yeah, bye, Ellie,' said Riley, flashing me a look that I knew too well. 'Bye, Cadence.'

'Bye!' Cadence trilled.

I watched Riley hurry after Paige and I felt my heart might break. I knew, from being the new girl in musical theatre, what it was like to think you had no friends or no one on your side. I didn't want my best friend Paige to feel like I didn't care about her or had forgotten about her just because I had finally started to fit in and make new friends.

Cadence was really nice, but there was no one like my Paige.

'Just a sec,' I said to Cadence.

I jumped down the steps and pelted after Paige and didn't stop until I'd wrapped her up in a big bear hug, and then I got Riley into it as well, for good measure.

'I missed you guys today,' I said. 'I hope you were extra mean to Jasmine for me.'

'Ellie, you're crushing my ribcage,' Riley complained, although she was smiling.

'Let's do something this afternoon, after I finish rehearsal,' I said. 'Ash, too. I have to tell you all about these pink and silver leg warmers I saw online. I would kill for them.'

'You're about to kill me right now by crushing me to death,' Riley wheezed.

'That sounds nice.' Paige smiled, finally looking at me.

'Bring the snakes,' I said, 'I'll need them.'

I gave them one last squeeze before I went back to Cadence and *Mary Poppins*.

New experiences and new friends are very cool and very exciting.

But there's nothing like the old ones.

Chapter Seventeen

'And, grab off, grab off, shuffle slap, hop hop, tap spring, tap spring, ball change, toe stamp!'

The last stamp sounded like a victory cry, as everyone collapsed and remembered to breathe again.

We were finally coming to the end of rehearsing our 'Step in Time' piece for the variety night.

Let's just say that even in my fastest jazz choreography, I had barely been as puffed as this. I'm surprised that any sound came out at all when I sang. Tapping was hard work! But, oh my gosh, the piece looked and sounded amazing.

We had our costumes! As I said, the tapping troupe for this number was dressed as chimney sweeps. This part of *Mary Poppins* is when Mary takes Jane and her brother up on the roof and Bert (the leader of the chimney sweeps) shows them that there is always a team of chimney sweeps up there watching out for them and being their guardian angels.

The rest of the cast (the adults) would come on too, giving depth to the singing when our ferocious tapping made it hard for us to really belt out the words. They acted as poor townspeople and just did some basic jazz. But the chimney sweeps were the real

stars! I'd even given my chimney sweep character a name, Charli, after my middle name, Charlotte.

For our costumes we had three-quarter black pantaloons held up by braces, with grey socks and our shiny new black taps. We also had little pageboy caps, neck kerchiefs and props – chimney sweeps that looked real but were actually made out of tulle so they would be extra light when we were dancing with them.

My favourite part of the costume, though, was the short-sleeved stripy top we wore underneath the braces. The boys had a maroon colour while the girls were decked out in a deep pink shade that would sparkle when we went under the lights.

Pink is my favourite colour, of course, so I took it as another good omen.

Cadence had great fun in dress rehearsal painting pretend soot and dirt on my face and arms, and teasing my hair into a big fluffy bird's nest.

'Don't forget your tooth!' She giggled, swiping some paint on one of my teeth.

'Cadence!' I protested, pretending to bite at one of her fingers.

'Oooh!' said Cadence. 'I knew chimney sweeps often went hungry, but I didn't know they were *that* hungry!'

'Ain't no meat on those dainty little digits anyway.' I mugged, talking in a cockney British accent like how I imagined my character would.

'Aah!' squealed Cadence. 'You're too believable!'

I chased her with the tub of black paint, threatening to dye her pretty red hair.

The dancing was so athletic, Periwinkle had outdone himself. We were doing constant side kicks, side leaps, tuck jumps and a lot of partner work where we would swing off and launch each other into the air.

It wasn't just jazzy musical theatre technical steps. After we finished each technique or trick, we then had to connect it to some kind of tap combination so that everything was fluid and linked together.

We even had a chorus line with Mary and Bert in the middle where we would tap up, kick forward then back, jump, lay out and add forward springs. I don't know about you, but trying to do that alone, much less connected to sixteen other people, is hard work!

The way we moved in rehearsal reminded me a bit of puppets being jigged up and down by giants up in the rafters, making us do the silliest things. At the start of the song when it was just Bert, Mary and the two kids on stage, and the song was building to its crescendo, all the chimney sweeps had to peep and clamber out of these chimney props and be very cheeky.

It was the best mix of acting, dancing and singing I could hope for! I was now a certified triple threat!

The final step, of course, was to pull off the perfect, most energetic performance.

Then I could rightly say that Broadway had better watch out, 'cause there was a new kid on the scene, and her name was Eleanor Irvin.

Chapter Eighteen

This *Mary Poppins* performance for variety night wasn't like any other performance I'd done in my time at Silver Shoes.

This was something that was mine, something that I'd pursued and worked hard for. It was me showing everyone that all my talk of the past few months was because of this; that the world of the stage was what I'd dreamed about and lived for.

So it was extra exciting. But it also made me extra nervous.

I was a mess backstage at the Entertainment Centre. I forgot my false eyelashes. And when I came back from the bathroom I thought I'd lost my *Mary Poppins* crew because there were so many other acts from other schools and companies rushing about and crowding the hallways.

When I tried to sing some quiet warm-up notes to myself, I felt like a frog had died in my throat. My voice sounded like a husky old ear of corn and no amount of clearing my throat made it better.

Then I couldn't get the braces to attach on my pants! They kept popping off and one sprang off, hit me in the neck and left an ugly red mark on my skin.

'Cadence!' I turned to her, my eyes all big and wet from the panicky tears that were threatening to ruin my moment.

Cadence, the pro, turned my way like she was twenty years older than me and not just a few months. 'Yes, Ellie?' she said.

I pointed at my neck, which was really meant to somehow sum up my whole freak-out. Lucky Cadence was smart as well as talented.

'Well, that's easy enough to disguise,' she said, reaching for a tub of greasepaint and painting over the red welt with one swipe of her fingers.

'Thank you,' I said, reaching for the snakes like my life depended on it.

'Okay,' said Cadence. 'I know how to fix this.' She grabbed my hand and pulled me stumbling out of the dressing room (one of my tap shoes was unbuckled and kept catching on my heel).

'Where are we going?' I asked through a mouthful of snakes.

'Ssshh,' said Cadence. 'Follow me. We're not supposed to be there, but no one's around at this time just before they open the house.'

'Where?' I asked. 'What?'

Cadence peeped over her shoulder before dashing up the steps to the backstage area and creeping through the cracked open door.

'Here.' She pulled me out through the dark silent wings to the empty stage, which was lit by one spotlight.

It was just like in my dreams. The dust motes floating through the air in their own secret dance. The rows of shadowy seats rising all the way to the back. The sweet musty smell of the curtains. The spotlight casting a warm yellow circle on the ground.

And me. Standing in the middle of my stage.

'This is all you need to think about and feel,' said Cadence, still holding my hand but using her other arm to sweep about. 'Fill every inch of this stage with what you love about performing. This is your world and it doesn't care about false eyelashes and braces marks. You're here to perform and entertain, because it's in your blood. So just listen to what your heart tells you.'

I looked out at the auditorium. 'Cadence,' I said softly, 'who told you that? That's exactly how I feel.'

'Sometimes,' said Cadence, '*you're* the only teacher you need and you just have to learn to listen to yourself.' She squeezed my hand. 'I'll leave you alone for a bit. The stage is all yours.'

'Thank you,' I said.

Her footsteps died away and I stood staring out at my pretend audience. I didn't make a sound and I felt very calm and peaceful.

Cadence was right. This was where I belonged and my blood and heart knew it, even if sometimes my mind didn't.

'Pssst,' I heard from the side.

I blinked.

'Ellie,' someone whispered. 'Over here!'

Dazed, I turned to my left and saw three familiar faces peering out at me from the wings. The smallest, blondest one was holding a big bouquet of sunflowers, my favourite.

'Quick,' Ashley hissed at me. 'We're not supposed to be back here but Cadence said this was where you would be. We brought you some flowers for your big debut!'

'And snakes,' Riley said from behind her.

'And hugs,' added Paige, holding out the bouquet.

I smiled. There were other things, not dance-related, that your heart and blood and mind could tell you.

And this time, I listened.

So You Think You Know Tap?

Fun facts about tap and musical theatre:

- Musical theatre is a form of theatrical performance that combines songs, spoken words, acting and dance. Musicals as we know them began to be popular in the first quarter of the 1900s. A lot of musical films you might have seen would have begun on the stage.

- The first dog to play Sandy in the original Broadway production of *Annie* was saved from a pound and made a star. From then on, traditionally every dog who played Sandy was rescued from the pound.

- Tap dancing is the fusion of British Isles clog and step dancing mixed with the rhythms of West African drumming. It began in the mid 1600s when Scottish and

Irish workmen brought their social dances to the United States of America, where it was copied by slaves.

- In the late 1800s, there were two tap techniques used: a fast style using wooden-soled shoes, and a smoother style using leather-soled shoes. By the 1920s they had merged when metal taps were introduced to the ball and heel of the dancer's shoe. Before that, people would often stick coins on the bottom of their shoes to make a louder sound!

- Hoofers are tap dancers who dance mostly with their legs, making a louder, more grounded sound. This kind of tap dancing is called 'rhythm tap'.

- 'Broadway tap' is more common these days, and is a fluid style influenced by early tappers like Fred Astaire, who added elements of ballroom, and Gene Kelly, who used his ballet training to give tap athleticism.

Famous tappers
- Fred Astaire
- Gene Kelly
- Bill 'Bojangles' Robinson
- Gregory Hines
- Savion Glover

Musicals with tap
- *Singin' in the Rain*
- *42nd Street*
- *Billy Elliot*
- *Mary Poppins*
- *All That Jazz*

Movies with tap
- *Chicago*
- *High School Musical*

- *Happy Feet*
- *Bootmen*
- *Stepping Out*

Glossary

Hey there, hoofers!

That is, of course, what they called tap dancers in the olden days. But tapping is just as much fun if you do it now! Here are some of the steps and musical terms you might come across when you first begin to learn tap – trust me, it's tricky first off, but if you do mine and Paige's trick of listening to the beats and letting your feet follow, it sure helps. Another great tip is that crisp, sharp taps are always better than just making the loudest sound you can. See you on Broadway, my beauties!

Love, Ellie

back brush one sound, a broad movement that swings from the hip and 'brushes' against the floor

ball change two sounds, shifting the weight from foot to foot (two steps)

ball dig one sound, the ball of the foot gives a sharp hard dig on the floor

grab off four sounds, lift your right foot then your left, and then ball change

mezzo-soprano the 'middle' vocal range between a soprano (high) and a contralto (low)

minim in music, a half note (two beats) with the stem facing up or down – it looks like this: ♩

pick up one sound, you stand on both feet, tilt up the toe of one foot and sharply tap back, removing your heel

repertoire a collection of songs, dances, choreography etc. that a person knows and can perform if they are called upon to do so

semibreve in music, a whole note (four beats) that looks like a hollow circle

side kicks straight leg kicks out to the side

shuffle two sounds, quick forward and back taps done to the count of one

shuffle toe heel turns three sounds, one direction; twelve sounds to do a whole turn – like a shuffle but you put your heel down after the shuffle and complete a full turn

slap two sounds, an ankle action where you tap forward and finish with a ball dig (keep your knees relaxed!)

slap ball change four sounds, you slap forward and shift your weight with a ball change

split jump splits in second position in the air

stamp one sound, a flat foot drop, just like you're stamping

tap spring two sounds, forward tap and then spring onto the ball (front) of the foot (like a hop)

time step seven sounds! A common step made up of stamps, springs, shuffles and slaps, the weight shifting from foot to foot

toe heel two sounds, a ball dig followed by you dropping your heel on the same foot

trenches five sounds, a scraping kind of movement with springs and heel drops, and can be done to the front (hoofer) or to the side (over-the-tops)

triple threat an all-round performer who can sing, dance and act very well

wings three sounds, you jump/hop, brushing both feet out and in and then coming together, so it looks like your feet are fluttering once

About the Author

Samantha-Ellen Bound has been an actor, dancer, teacher, choreographer, author, bookseller, scriptwriter and many other things besides. She has published and won prizes for her short stories and scripts, but children's books are where her heart lies. Dancing is one of her most favourite things in the whole world. She splits her time between Tasmania, Melbourne, and living in her own head.

Silver Shoes

Rhythm and Blues

SAMANTHA-ELLEN BOUND

AVAILABLE JANUARY 2016

AVAILABLE JANUARY 2016

COLLECT THEM ALL!